Happy Birthday to *Whooo?*

By Doris Fisher   Illustrated by Lisa Downey

For my mother, Emily Todd Lewis, and in memory of my father, John C. Lewis – DF
For my husband, Len, and in loving memory of Agnes Knudson – LD
Thanks to educators at the Houston Zoo for verifying the accuracy of
the information in this book.

Library of Congress Control Number: 2005931003
ISBN 13: 978-0-9768823-1-2
ISBN 10: 0-9768823-1-0
Copyright © 2006 by Sylvan Dell Publishing
Printed in China

Sylvan Dell Publishing
976 Houston Northcutt Blvd., Suite 3
Mt. Pleasant, SC 29464

www.SylvanDellPublishing.com

Everyone has a birthday.
Parents celebrate each new baby.
Can you guess the baby animal
from the clues in
these announcements?

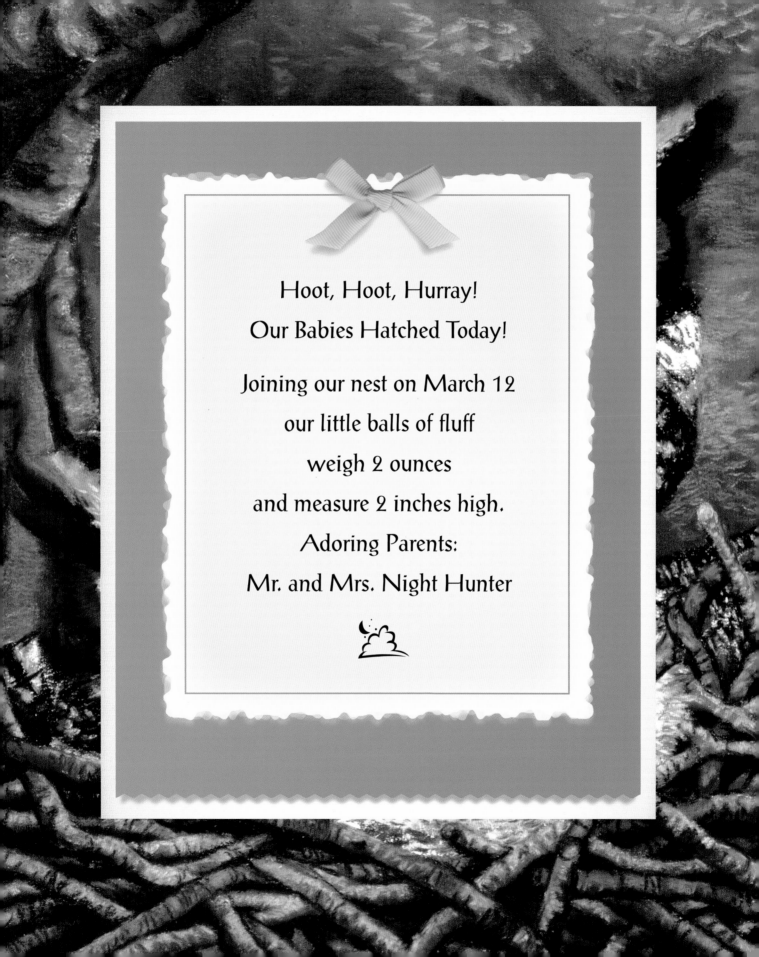

Hoot, Hoot, Hurray!
Our Babies Hatched Today!

Joining our nest on March 12
our little balls of fluff
weigh 2 ounces
and measure 2 inches high.
Adoring Parents:
Mr. and Mrs. Night Hunter

A baby owl walks and hops on tree branches until it learns to fly.

Our Pride Has Arrived!

Triplet cubs born on June 20
to Mr. and Mrs. Jung L. King.

Our babies weigh

1½ pounds each

and measure 12 inches.

Lion cubs practice pouncing and playing to learn how to hunt.

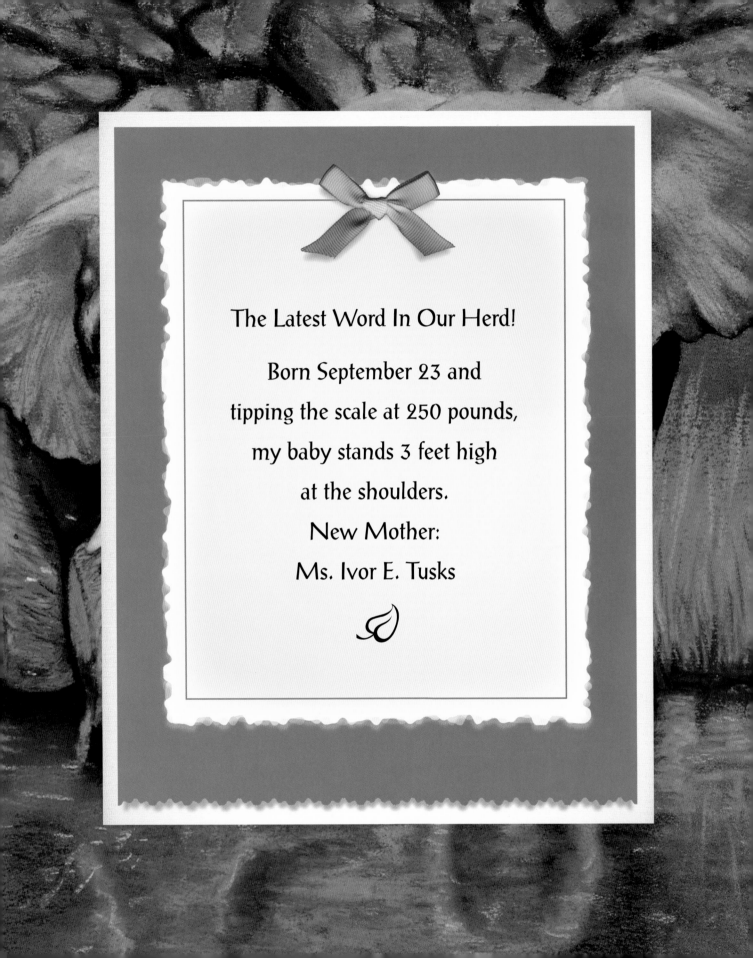

The Latest Word In Our Herd!

Born September 23 and
tipping the scale at 250 pounds,
my baby stands 3 feet high
at the shoulders.
New Mother:
Ms. Ivor E. Tusks

A baby elephant uses its trunk to touch
and explore its world.

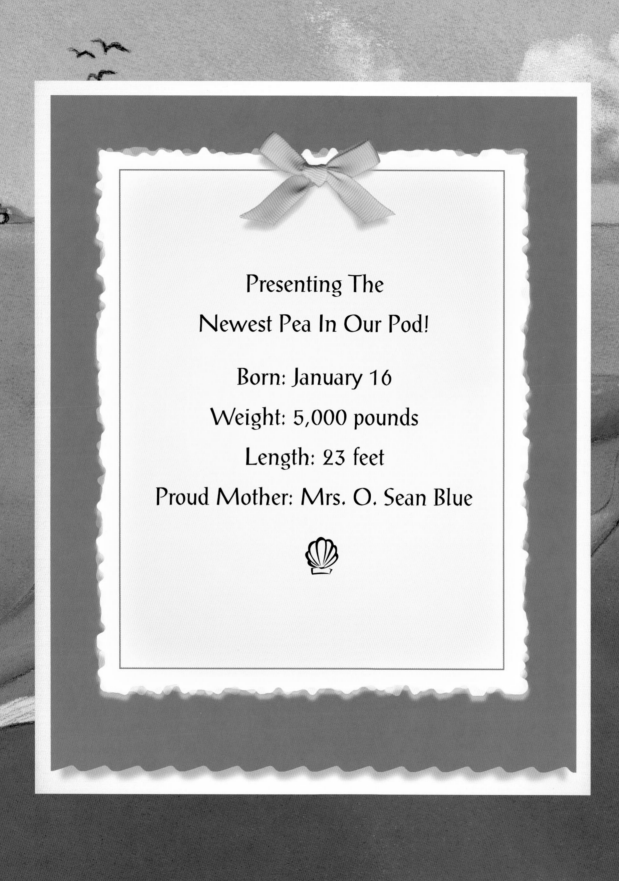

Presenting The
Newest Pea In Our Pod!

Born: January 16

Weight: 5,000 pounds

Length: 23 feet

Proud Mother: Mrs. O. Sean Blue

A baby blue whale drinks enough milk to gain 200 pounds every day for the first few weeks.

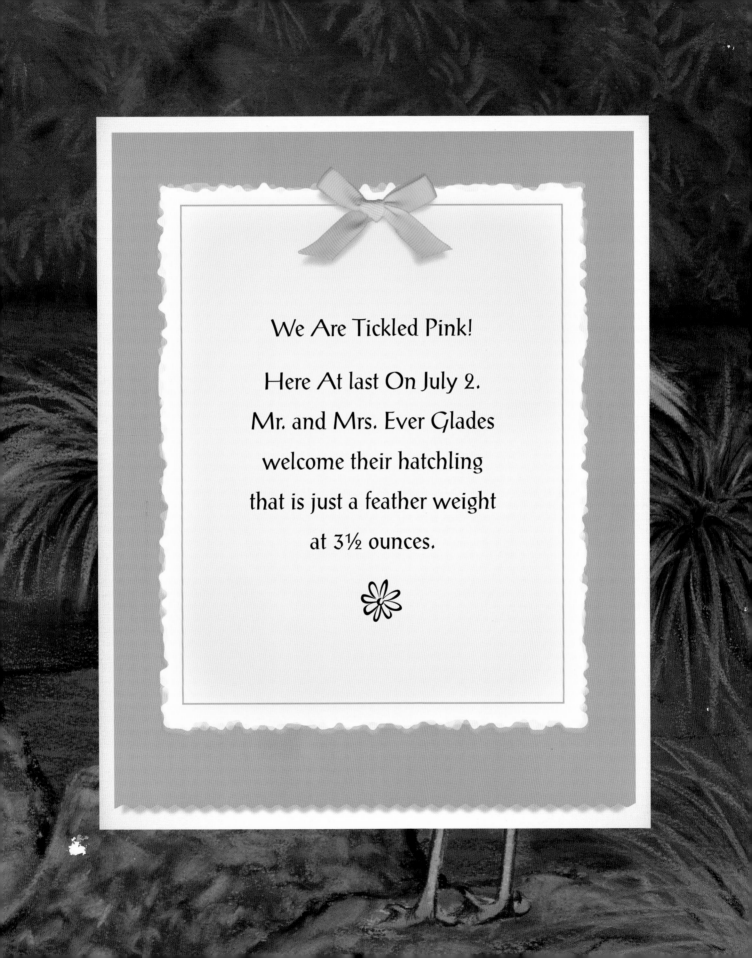

We Are Tickled Pink!

Here At last On July 2.
Mr. and Mrs. Ever Glades
welcome their hatchling
that is just a feather weight
at 3½ ounces.

A baby flamingo has gray and white feathers which gradually turn pink in three years.

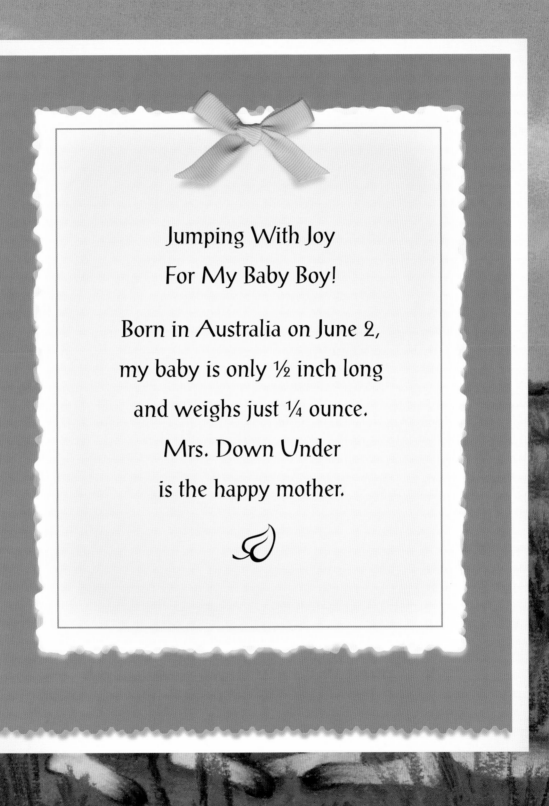

Jumping With Joy
For My Baby Boy!

Born in Australia on June 2,
my baby is only ½ inch long
and weighs just ¼ ounce.
Mrs. Down Under
is the happy mother.

A baby kangaroo grows inside its mother's pouch and is called a Joey.

Say Hello To
Our Spitting Image!

Born on April 21,
our new baby weighs 100 pounds
and is almost 4 feet tall.
Thrilled Parents:
Mr. and Mrs. O. A. Sis

A baby camel has thick eyelashes to keep
sand from blowing into its eyes.

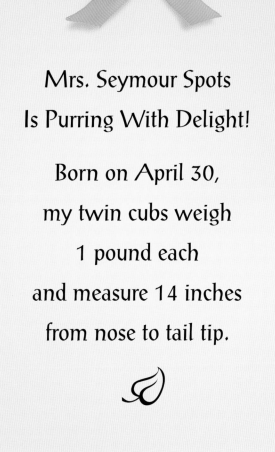

Mrs. Seymour Spots
Is Purring With Delight!

Born on April 30,
my twin cubs weigh
1 pound each
and measure 14 inches
from nose to tail tip.

Baby leopards like to climb, jump, and play—just like pet cats!

Welcoming My Baby
With Head Held High!

Born: October 6

Weight: 150 pounds

Height: 6 feet

Pleased Mother: Mrs. On Stilts

By the time a baby giraffe is one
year old, it stands 10 feet tall.

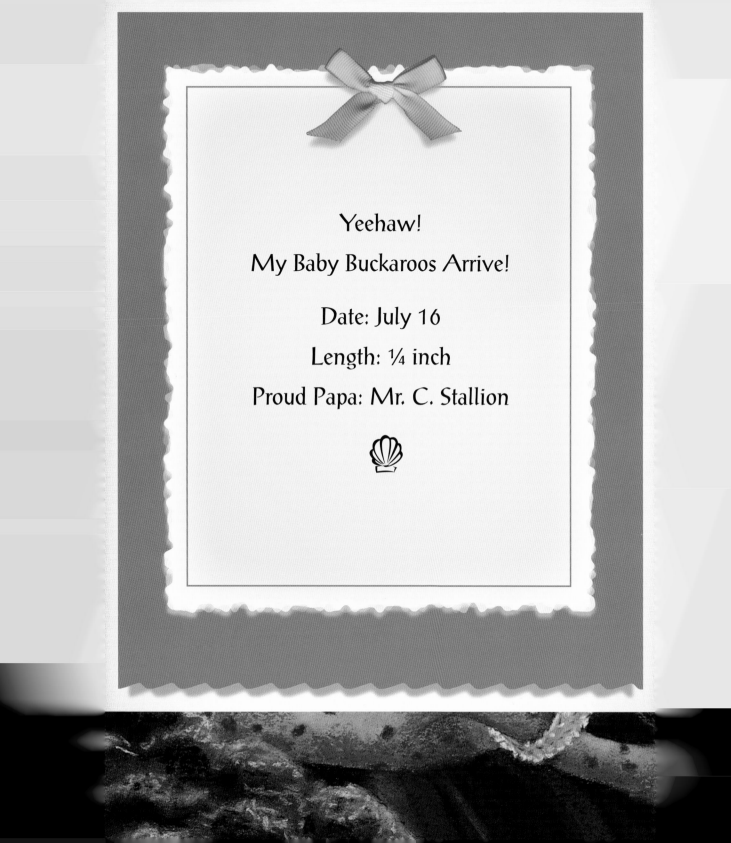

Yeehaw!

My Baby Buckaroos Arrive!

Date: July 16

Length: ¼ inch

Proud Papa: Mr. C. Stallion

The seahorse dad gives birth to between 50 to 200 fry at a time, depending on the species.

Celebrating Four Little Stinkers!

My babies are born
on May 16,
weighing 1 ounce each,
and measuring 4 inches long.
Proud mother: Mrs. P.U. Smell

Baby skunks can use their stinky
spray at 7 weeks.

We Are Soaring High
In The Sky!

Born on May 10,
our new baby weighs 3 ounces,
and is 3 inches high.
Excited Parents:
Mr. and Mrs. Keen I. Sight

A baby eagle is fed small bits of meat by both parents and is called an eaglet.

For Creative Minds

Animal Families

Babies are born in all different sizes and shapes. Animal babies are also cared for in many different ways. Some babies are cared for by both their parents, some by just their mother, some by their father, and some by groups of moms, aunts, and grandmothers. There are even some animals who never know their parents; they survive on instinct. Some babies live with their family for just a few days, months, or years. Or some, like female dolphins or elephants may live with their family for their entire lives. *Read the announcements and the fun facts to identify which animals are cared for by a family like yours.*

Animal Fun Facts

Great Horned Owls

The parents use the empty nest of another animal or bird, like a crow's or a hawk's, for their own nest.

Both parents are involved in raising the young.

A mother usually lays two or three eggs at a time.

They are nocturnal and hunt and eat small animals.

Lions

A pride of lions consists of 2 to 18 lions, a few males, females and their offspring.

The cubs nurse from their mother or any of the females (lionesses) in their group or crèche.

Male lions eat first, while the lionesses and cubs wait their turns.

The cubs like to lick and play.

Male cubs start to grow a mane, their shaggy, hairy collar, when they are about two years old. When the manes are fully grown, the males are fully mature and must leave the pride.

Lions are crepuscular and nocturnal. That means that they are most active at dawn and dusk (when they do most of their hunting) and that they are awake at night. *When are you most active and when do you sleep – day or night?*

Elephants

An elephant calf drinks about three gallons of milk a day when nursing. *How many gallons of milk does your family drink in a day? Is it more or less than a baby elephant?*

A calf may suck its trunk like a human child sucks its thumb.

The adults in a herd of elephants are all females: mother, grandmothers, and aunts.

Male babies live in the herd with the females until they are about 12 years old. Then they live alone or with other males. Occasionally they visit the female herds.

Blue Whales

A baby blue whale starts to eat krill when it is about six months old.

A baby blue whale is called a calf.

Blue whales are often seen alone, in pairs, or in small groups called pods.

A fully-grown blue whale can be as large as two or three school buses parked in front of each other. They are the largest animals on earth.

Flamingos

Both the male and female build the nest and care for the young.

They may stay together as a "couple" for several years.

A baby is called a chick or a nestling.

The chick leaves the nest when it is five to eight days old.

It joins a group of other chicks, called a crèche.

Flamingos have 12 primary flight feathers on each wing.

They have 19 vertebrae (bones) in their necks for flexibility compared to the seven vertebrae in the necks of humans and giraffes.

Kangaroos

Kangaroos live in groups called "mobs."

Females are called does, flyers, or jills.

Males are called bucks, jacks, or boomers.

Joeys are the size of a jellybean when they are born.

A kangaroo is a marsupial, an animal whose young lives in a pouch.

A joey lives inside its mother's pouch for 6 to 10 months.

Kangaroos can jump over objects that are as high as six feet.

They are crepuscular and nocturnal, which means they are most active at dusk and dawn, are awake at night, and sleep during the day.

Camels

Baby camels are called calves and may weigh between 80 and 130 pounds at birth.

They can stand after two or three hours.

They generally nurse for one year.

The calves stay with their mothers about four years.

Camels store fat in their humps and can go for several days without drinking.

They can drink 50 gallons of water in less than an hour if it is hot and they have been without water. *How many (8 oz.) cups of water do you normally drink a day? How many cups are in a gallon? How many cups in 50 gallons?*

Leopards

Leopards live alone. They are solitary animals.

Leopards can run short distances at 36 miles per hour (mph). *Next time you are in a car, see how fast 36 mph is; can you run that fast?*

They can jump forward 20 feet or up to 10 feet high in the air.

A female can have one to three cubs at a time, but usually has two.

The cubs live with their mother until they are about 18 months old. Then they go off on their own.

Giraffes

A baby giraffe is called a calf.

It can stand up when it is about one hour old. *How old were you when you could stand or walk?*

Giraffe mothers may take turns watching a group of babies.

They are plant eaters and love to eat the leaves off trees.

The tall neck is designed to reach high into the trees but it only has seven bones (vertebrae), the same as we have!

A herd of giraffes may consist of males, females, and calves.

Male giraffes leave the herd when they are about four years old.

Seahorses

A seahorse is a type of fish.

The mom deposits her eggs into the dad's special pouch. It is actually the dad that gives birth to the babies!

Seahorses' eyes move in different directions from each other so they can see all around.

They are not good swimmers.

They hold onto coral or plants with their tails.

Their tube-like mouth is used like a vacuum cleaner to suck in their food.

Skunks

Baby skunks are called kits and are blind when they are born.

The kits stay in the burrow or nest until they are about six weeks old.

After six weeks, the kits follow their mother when hunting and will stay with her through the summer.

They head out on their own in the fall.

Eagles

A pair of bald eagles mates for life and raises their young together.

Eagles usually use the same nest year after year.

An average eagle nest is five feet in diameter.

Bald Eagles have 7,000 feathers!

It's a numbers game!

Copy and cut out each animal graphic on this page. Using poster board cut into long strips and taped together or using chalk on a driveway, sidewalk, or playground; measure and draw a number line that is six feet long. Place each animal graphic on the number that represents the height or length of each animal baby mentioned in the book. If space permits, walk the distance of the size of a baby blue whale.

Make Your Own Birth Announcement

Who is the newest member of your family? Is it you? Is it a new brother or sister? Or, is it a new kitten or puppy? Compare the birth information of your new family member to some of the other animals in this book. Use the template on this page to design your own announcement. Try to use hints for people to guess who or what the newest member of your family is.

Welcome To The Newest Member Of Our Family!

Name: _____

Date: _____

Weight: _____

Length: _____

Delighted Family Members:

_____